DISNEY fairies

Trill Changes Her Tune

Trill Changes Her Tune

WRITTEN BY
GAIL HERMAN

ILLUSTRATED BY
DENISE SHIMABUKURO, LOREN CONTRERAS
& DEE FARNSWORTH

RANDOM HOUSE 🏠 NEW YORK

Library of Congress Cataloging-in-Publication Data

Herman, Gail.

Trill changes her tune / written by Gail Herman ; illustrated by
Denise Shimabukuro, Loren Contreras & Dee Farnsworth. — 1st ed.

p. cm. — (Disney fairies)

Summary: After losing her panpipes, shy Trill convinces some other
music-talent fairies to try less traditional instruments in the
upcoming Oceanside Symphony concert.

ISBN 978-0-7364-2660-2 (pbk.)

[1. Fairies—Fiction. 2. Musical instruments—Fiction. 3. Bashfulness—Fiction.]
I. Shimabukuro, Denise, ill. II. Contreras, Loren, ill.
III. Farnsworth, Dee, ill. IV. Title.

PZ7.H04315Tri 2011

[Fic]—dc22   2010022541

www.randomhouse.com/kids

Printed in the United States of America

10 9 8 7 6 5 4 3 2 1

All About Fairies

IF YOU HEAD toward the second star on your right and fly straight on till morning, you'll come to Never Land, a magical island where mermaids play and children never grow up.

When you arrive, you might hear something like the tinkling of little bells. Follow that sound and you'll find Pixie Hollow, the secret heart of Never Land.

A great old maple tree grows in Pixie

Hollow, and in it live hundreds of fairies and sparrow men. Some of them can do water magic, others can fly like the wind, and still others can speak to animals. You see, Pixie Hollow is the Never fairies' kingdom, and each fairy who lives there has a special, extraordinary talent.

Not far from the Home Tree, nestled in the branches of a hawthorn, is Mother Dove, the most magical creature of all. She sits on her egg, watching over the fairies, who in turn watch over her. For as long as Mother Dove's egg stays well and whole, no one in Never Land will ever grow old.

Once, Mother Dove's egg *was* broken. But we are not telling the story of the egg here. Now it is time for Trill's tale. . . .

Trill
Changes
Her
Tune

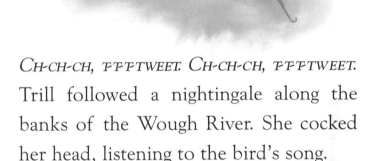

CH-CH-CH, T-T-TWEET. CH-CH-CH, T-T-TWEET.
Trill followed a nightingale along the banks of the Wough River. She cocked her head, listening to the bird's song.

Trill was a music-talent fairy. She heard music in every corner of Never Land. She always found a melody, a beat, or a rhythm wherever she went. Right now it was the nightingale chirping, singing a duet with the rush of the river.

"How lovely!" Trill murmured. She settled on the branch of a birch tree, just below the one the bird had landed on.

Quietly, Trill slipped off her leaf-

pack and took out her instrument, the panpipes.

The panpipes were made from hollow bamboo shoots glued together with sap and tied with vines. To Trill, they felt as light and comfortable as her very own wings.

Trill blew across the pipes, warming up. Each shoot was a different length and sounded a different note.

Whoooo. Toot, toot, whoooo. The notes flowed into one another. The lilting music echoed through the trees, over the water.

T-t-t-tweet, the nightingale sang. *Sh-sh-sh,* the water gurgled. *Tootle-whooo,* Trill played.

Beck and Fawn, two animal talents,

fluttered up to the branch. "That sounds nice!" said Beck.

Trill blushed, and her glow turned a deep orange. She ducked her head. Her long, unruly curls covered her face. "I—I—I didn't know anyone was listening!"

Beck sat down and swung her legs back and forth. "Well, we were just flying by. We're meeting some chipmunks for an acorn hunt. You know, Trill, you can come, too."

"Yes! Come!" said Fawn.

Trill thought for a moment. Sometimes chipmunk chatter had a chirping beat. Almost like a bird's song . . .

But if she went with Beck and Fawn, she'd have to think of things to say.

Trill liked Beck. She liked Fawn, too.

But she didn't know them very well. What would she talk about? Probably she'd wind up saying nothing at all and just getting in the way.

"N-n-nooo." Trill shook her head. She hunched over a bit so that she and Beck were eye to eye. Trill was taller than the average fairy. But she never liked to stand out. "Maybe another time."

"Sure, another time," Beck said easily. "Fly with you later!"

The animal talents took off. Trill watched as they fluttered close to the ground, calling out to the chipmunks.

Alone again, Trill let out a breath.

Good thing I didn't go, she thought. The whole idea—being with other talents! Doing something she'd never done! She felt nervous just thinking about it!

Trill swung her legs back and forth, the way Beck had done. Still, it might have been fun. Sometimes she wished she weren't so shy.

Trill picked up the panpipes again and began to play. Soon she was lost in the music. It blended with the rumble of the water . . . the rustling of leaves . . . the occasional croak or twitter. Trill yawned, lulled by the soft sounds.

I could stay here all day, she thought.

The panpipes slipped from her hands. Her eyelids drooped. *Zzzz*. Her soft snores mixed with the sounds of the woods.

Bzzzz. A bee buzzed by Trill's ear.

Trill sat up with a start. "Uh-oh!" How long had she been sleeping? She gazed through the trees. The sun hung low in the sky.

She *had* been here all day. Well, all afternoon, at least.

Trill was due back at the Home Tree. The music talents were meeting in the courtyard to plan the upcoming Ocean-side Symphony.

I can't be late for that! Trill thought. *Cleff's in charge.*

Cleff was always the first music talent at any meeting, at any concert—at anything at all. Even when he had the fairy flu, he came to the tearoom for every meal, right on time.

Trill dove from the branch. She

swooped along the muddy riverbank. Then she zoomed toward the Home Tree.

Ch-ch-chirp! Ch-ch-chirp! That wasn't another bird singing . . . was it?

Trill paused.

No! Two river otters were sliding down the muddy bank, a mother and her baby. They cooed, whistled, and chirped.

Was Beck close by? Or Fawn? No. No one would hear her. "*Hmmmmmmm, hmmmm,*" Trill hummed along.

Then the baby dove into the water. Trill hovered over the river, waiting for more of his music.

Ch-ch-chirp! Right below Trill, the otter came up for air. He looked her in the eye.

Trill held her breath. The otter opened his mouth.

"*Eeeeeee!*" He screamed for his mother. His cry was so loud, it was earsplitting! Trill fell backward in surprise. Her wings dropped into the river.

"Oh, no!" she moaned. She'd gotten her wings wet!

Already, she felt the wings weigh her down. She beat them furiously. But they were heavy from the water. They hardly moved at all.

Trill flew low, struggling to keep above the river. Like most fairies, she couldn't swim. She had to reach the shore! But she was sinking fast.

Her toes dipped into the river, then her knees. The water lapped at her waist, then reached up to her leaf-pack. She dropped lower . . . lower . . .

Her feet touched the river floor. The water was only inches deep.

Panting a bit, Trill pulled herself to shore. "*Brrrr.*" She shivered. The air felt cold. And she couldn't fly. Her wings were too damp.

But it was almost time for the symphony meeting. She had to get to the Home Tree—now!

Trill trudged through the woods, climbing over roots and skirting tall plants.

If she hurried, if she really, really rushed, maybe she'd get to the meeting on time.

2

AT LAST, TRILL reached the Home Tree. She stopped just outside the courtyard and craned her neck to see through the bushes into the yard.

All the music talents sat on pebbles, grouped around Cleff. They were looking up at him, waiting.

Tap, tap, tap. Cleff drummed his foot against the paving stoves. He glanced at the sun, which was just dipping below the horizon. Then he shook his head.

Cleff hadn't started the meeting yet, Trill realized. *He looks as if he's waiting for someone,* she thought in a panic. *Probably me!*

Trill wanted to rush in. She wanted to explain why she was late. But then all the musicians would stare at her. So she stayed hidden behind the bushes.

Tap, tap, tap. Cleff sighed and finally spoke. "I'd like to call this meeting to order. As you all know, we're here to discuss the Oceanside Symphony."

He turned to point in the direction of the shore.

This was Trill's chance! There was an empty pebble next to her best friend, Cadence. Holding her breath, Trill

parted the leaves of the bushes. Then she slipped in among the music talents.

Would Cleff notice?

"Oh, there you are, Trill," Cleff said as he turned back around. Everyone twisted in their seats to look at her.

Cleff didn't sound annoyed or angry. Still, Trill's glow burned deep orange.

"I—I—I know I'm l-l-late," she said. Oh, why did she have to stutter when she was nervous! And why did she have to tower over the other fairies and sparrow men? She was always so . . . so noticeable!

Trill shrank down low on her seat. "I'd fly b-b-backward if I could."

She didn't want to say any more. *But*

maybe, she thought, *I should tell Cleff about the otter? And about getting wet?*

Cleff didn't ask for any explanation, though. He nodded and went on. "As I was saying, the Oceanside Symphony will be held three nights from now. It's coming right up. We need to . . ."

As Cleff spoke, Cadence patted Trill's hand. Grateful, Trill smiled at her friend.

I'll pay close attention now, Trill promised herself. *I'll be a model music talent.*

It wouldn't be difficult, she thought. She loved the Oceanside Symphony. The concert was held on a clear moonlit night. Dulcie and the baking talents pre-pared a grand feast. And the light talents ended the evening with a magnificent light show.

Best of all, the sound of the breaking waves blended with the music. It was all so wonderful!

"We'll begin with 'Welcome One, Welcome All,'" Cleff read from his notes, "and end with 'Fare Thee Well, Sweet Moon and Stars.' There'll be three additional pieces. The crickets will join in on the . . ."

Trill's mind wandered. She could guess everything Cleff would say. For as long as she could remember, every symphony had been the same. The same songs. The same order. True, the feast and the lights were amazing. And the music, too, of course.

Trill loved performing in concerts. Whenever she played with other musicians, anytime, anywhere, she felt comfortable. Holding her panpipes, she was almost graceful. She didn't mind other fairies looking at her at all.

Still, the Oceanside Symphony was becoming . . . not boring, exactly. Trill wouldn't say that. Predictable? Yes, that was it.

"Ahem." Cleff cleared his throat. Then he unrolled a long scroll. The leaf-paper was covered with complicated drawings of driftwood seats and musicians' names. Arrows pointed every which way.

"This shows who sits where, and who plays when," Cleff explained.

Everyone shifted closer to see.

"The trumpeters and percussionists will sit closest to the water," Cleff said. "The harpists and others, farther back."

Didn't they always sit this way? Trill sighed as Cleff went on and on.

Sh-sh-sh. A soft sound wafted out

through an open window. Trill peeked inside the Home Tree, into the lobby. Polishing talents were buffing the long, curving banister. Each time they swiped their moss rags, a shushing sound drifted into the courtyard.

"It's a rhythm!" Trill whispered to herself. She tapped her foot against the ground, adding a beat. Her fingers snapped in time. She closed her eyes.

"*Hmmmm, hmm,*" she hummed. Slowly, she felt a shift in the air. She opened one eye, then the other. Everyone was staring at her!

"Trill," said Cleff. He sounded as if this wasn't the first time he'd called her name. "What do you think about the change?"

Change? Trill looked at him, alert. "There's something new?" she asked.

"I was thinking the panpipe section should sit on the left," Cleff explained. He held up the scroll again. "That would mean the percussionists would move to the right, and the . . ."

Trill nodded absently. Did it really matter if she sat on the left or the right? The music was what counted. Everything else—the seating, the programs, the dresses—had its place, of course. But when it came right down to it, fairies were there for the music.

But Trill didn't want to question Cleff. Everyone would stare at her again. Besides, there were so many other interesting things to listen to. Trill focused on the tinkling of glasses coming from the kitchen. The banging of pots. The murmur of the breeze . . .

"All right, everyone," Cleff finally said. "I think we've covered everything. You've been very patient."

All around, fairies and sparrow men stood and stretched. Twins Ariette and Lyra brushed dirt from their dresses at the same exact time, in the same exact way.

Trill turned toward Cadence. "I have to tell you why I was—"

"Trill?" Cleff fluttered beside her. "Could you stay a bit longer?"

Trill gulped. Was Cleff going to scold her for being late? Would she be able to explain?

"I'd like to go over the panpipes solo in the third song."

Trill let out a breath. Finally! Something important! "Sure." She reached into her leaf-pack.

The panpipes weren't there!

3

"My panpipes! They're gone!" Trill cried. "Oh, no! I must have dropped them when I fell asleep!" Without another word to Cleff or Cadence, she took off for the Wough River.

"Wait! I'll come with you!" called Cadence.

Trill waited for her friend. Then, together, they flew to the riverbank to search.

"I've got to find them!" Trill darted down among the plants and shrubs, and up to the leafy treetops. "I've had them since I Arrived!"

Trill's panpipes had been made by the instrument master, Strad. The fairy had spent weeks crafting the bamboo shoots, hoping that a new Arrival would announce her talent and be a match for the instrument. And then Trill came to Never Land.

Trill knew she was a music talent right away, of course. Still, she felt lost at first, unsure of what she should do and where she should go. But then she held the panpipes and everything seemed right.

"I know exactly how you feel!" said

Cadence, trying to keep up. "If I lost my drums, I'd feel just awful."

The fairies peeked into a hollow log, then under a root.

"Are you looking for something?" Beck asked them. She waved good-bye to a seagull and flew over to Trill.

"Yes. My p-p-panpipes," said Trill. She was beginning to feel desperate. "I must have dropped them somewhere around here."

"I'll help," Beck offered. She circled the trees for a few minutes, searching. As she flew, she chattered in a strange high voice.

A chipmunk poked his head out of a nearby knothole, and Beck said something to him. Trill held her breath.

Maybe the chipmunk had seen her panpipes!

The animal shook his head and popped back into the hole.

"Oh! He doesn't know, either!" Trill said. She couldn't believe her panpipes might be gone forever.

"Don't give up!" Beck said. She pulled Trill and Cadence along as she flew to another tree. The fairies landed on a branch covered with brown and green leaves.

For a moment, no one moved.

Why were they just sitting here, doing nothing? "B-B-Beck—" Trill began.

"Shhh!" Beck made a noise deep in her throat. It sounded like sheets of sandpaper rubbing together. Slowly, two brown leaves unfurled.

"Oh!" Trill gasped. Those weren't leaves. It was a gray moth, opening her wings.

The moth bent toward Beck, making those same scratchy sounds.

"Did the moth see the panpipes?"

Cadence asked. "Does she know where they are?"

"No," Beck said.

Trill's heart dropped. What if they were really and truly gone? But Beck was already hopping off the branch. "Let's ask this blue jay!" she suggested.

Beck chirped, then listened to the bird's answer.

"She said to follow her!" Beck told Trill and Cadence.

The three fairies trailed the blue jay to a tall pine tree.

"We looked here already," Trill said. "The p-p-panpipes aren't here."

"Are you sure?" Beck landed next to the bird's nest and studied it closely.

"I see them!" Trill's voice rose in

excitement. "They're right there, in the nest!"

The blue jay had woven the panpipes in with twigs and leaves. Unless you looked closely, the panpipes were hard to spot—just like the moth resting among the leaves.

Carefully, Beck freed the panpipes. She patted the blue jay in thanks. Then she handed the instrument to Trill.

"Oh, I'm so happy!" Trill couldn't stop smiling. She had her panpipes back!

Cadence bent down to look at the instrument closely. "Uh-oh," she said.

Trill lifted the panpipes. They were scratched and muddied and knocked out of shape.

"They'll be fine," she said.

Trill had her instrument back. So what if it was a little damaged? How bad could it be?

"Listen." She blew into the shortest pipe.

BLAT! Trill winced at the noise. She blew into another pipe, then another. *BLAT! BLEAT!* Each note sounded terrible, like nails scraping against slate rock.

Uh-oh was right.

4

A LITTLE LATER, Trill waited quietly in Strad's workshop. She breathed in the smell of wood and sap and silk and felt a little better.

Instruments had their own special scents, and just sitting in the place where they were made and repaired soothed Trill.

She gazed around the room. Mini-pumpkins lined a set of walnut shelves. Next to those lay a pile of maple leaves. She knew the pumpkins would be carved into drums, and the leaves used as covers. Silk strings for fiddles and harps hung on thorn hooks. Coconut shells, filled with trumpet flowers, stood in every corner.

Trill turned toward Strad. The instrument maker sat on a stool, bent over her panpipes. Trill had been trying *not* to watch. She didn't want to see Strad's expression, or the way she toiled over the panpipes. Not seeing made it easy to believe that the panpipes would be fine.

"*Tsk, tsk.*" Strad clucked her tongue.

"Yes?" said Trill. She was so worried!

Strad touched one long dent that stretched across the top of the pipes. "That's a major problem right there. Everything else is just a matter of sanding and cleaning. But it will all take time."

"How much time?" Trill asked. "Will the panpipes be ready for the concert?"

Strad shrugged. "Maybe yes, maybe no. I can't make any promises."

Trill pointed to a shelf of panpipes on the other side of the workshop. "What about those? If you don't finish in time, can I use one?"

"Use one of these? Ha!" Strad strode across the room and grabbed an armful of panpipes. Then she let them clatter to the ground.

"They're all useless." She picked one

up and blew into it. It sounded like a foghorn. Another sounded like an owl screeching. "I just keep them for the day when I finally have time to try to fix them."

Strad moved close to Trill. "Besides, your instrument is a beauty. A work of art, if I do say so myself. You need to wait."

Wait? Trill swallowed. The Oceanside Symphony wouldn't wait because of one damaged instrument. She needed her panpipes now!

Trill had to find Cleff. *He should know about my panpipes,* she realized. But what would he say? Would he understand?

Trill hated to tell anyone bad news.

And this was very, very bad news. Cleff had everything planned, right down to the smallest detail. Surely he'd blame her for the mishap.

Trill left Strad's workshop and flew around Pixie Hollow, looking for Cleff. She moved slowly and a little unsteadily. Usually, her panpipes were at her side. Without them, she felt awkward and off balance.

Finally, Trill heard Cleff's voice. It was coming from the orange crate that art-talent Bess had turned into a studio. Trill peeked between the slats and listened.

"I thought we could put up a painting in the tearoom," Cleff was saying to Bess. "Something that would get everyone excited about the concert. You could paint a portrait. Maybe the musicians at the beach, or—"

Cleff frowned and lifted a foot. He'd stepped in a puddle of red berry paint.

Jars and jars of paints and brushes cluttered the studio. Old, used canvases and brand-new ones were scattered along the walls. The room was a mess. Cleff kept glancing around, looking uneasy.

He's so particular about things, Trill thought.

This would be a terrible moment to tell him about the panpipes. Most likely, he felt anxious already, just trying to avoid all the jumble. But time was running out. She didn't want to surprise him at the last minute.

"You do know that the flower trumpets are always pink blooms with white stripes?" Cleff asked Bess. "Not white flowers with pink stripes?"

Bess nodded.

Taking a deep breath, Trill fluttered into the studio, but she banged her head against the door frame. She ducked lower and blushed. More than anything, she wanted to turn and leave. But she forced herself to stay.

Cleff and Bess turned to her, looking curious.

"I—I—I don't mean to interrupt," Trill said.

"That's all right, Trill," Bess said.

"Are you here to see me?" Cleff asked.

"Yes." Trill paused. She stared at the floor, then explained everything in a rush.

Cleff pulled a lily pad out of his pocket to make a note. "Well, Trill. Let's hope your panpipes are ready in time. But we can only wait and see."

Trill sighed with relief. Cleff sounded surprised, disappointed, and a little bit frustrated. But certainly not angry.

"I'll fly with you later," Trill said, turning to leave.

Swish, swish. Trill froze in place. What was that sound?

Bess was sweeping a brush across a canvas, showing Cleff an outline of what she could paint. Trill listened harder. What a lovely rhythm!

The paintbrush was a stick, like a drumstick. What if the percussionists used a paintbrush, with the brush end striking the drum? Would it make a swishing sound, too? And could it make the music more interesting?

"Cleff?" In her excitement, Trill spoke without thinking or worrying. "What would you say to using paintbrushes for drumsticks? It could be something special for the concert. It would add a whole new sound!"

Cleff was eyeing Bess's outline, not really paying attention. His elbow grazed an empty paint jar and it clattered to the ground. He reached to pick it up and knocked over another one.

"Paintbrushes? Drumsticks?" he said

testily. "What are you talking about, Trill?"

Trill stepped back. "N-n-nothing," she stammered.

Quickly, Cleff righted the jars. "Now, will this painting be ready by sunrise?" he asked Bess.

When Bess said yes, he nodded at both fairies and left.

"Bess?" Trill said, hesitating a bit. "Can I borrow some of these brushes?"

"Look at these, Cadence!" Trill said excitedly. Trill and Cadence were in Trill's room. The windows were flung open, letting in the sounds of Pixie Hollow.

All around the bedroom, Trill had placed shell-horns and rhythm sticks and rattle-gourds. She even had an old drum she used for a nightstand tucked into a corner.

Cadence wrinkled her nose. "Paintbrushes!" she said. "You pulled me away from dinner to show me a bunch of paintbrushes?"

"Not just paintbrushes," Trill told her. She rolled the drum to the center of the room. "Drumsticks! Try them."

Cadence gave Trill a funny look. She struck the drum with the wooden end of the paintbrush. *Boom!* "So?" She shrugged. "It's just like using a regular drumstick."

"Wait," said Trill. She took the

paintbrushes from her friend, turned them over, and handed them back. "Try it again. Use the brush end."

Cadence tapped the drum. *Shh-boom.* "Hey!" she cried, delighted. "It has more of a ring. The vibration lasts longer."

Shh-boom, shh-boom. Cadence struck

the drum a bit harder. "And the sound is softer than using regular sticks, too."

Cadence kept playing. "This is great! It's a whole new sound! I know the other drummers will love it." She hugged Trill tight. "Do you think we can use these in the symphony?"

"I'm not sure," said Trill. "Cleff's in charge."

When she'd suggested the paint-brushes earlier, Cleff had pretty much ignored the idea. But maybe he'd had too much on his mind just then.

The drum sounds were new and different. And Cadence hadn't felt sure about the paintbrushes, either—until she'd tried them.

Just thinking of talking to Cleff

made Trill's heart beat quickly. This wasn't just any old idea. It was her idea. Did she dare bring it up again?

Yes! She had to try.

5

THE NEXT MORNING, Trill tucked the
paintbrushes under her arm and hurried
to the tearoom.

I'll go talk to Cleff right now, she
thought. She felt nervous. But maybe
they'd have a nice, friendly discussion
over breakfast. And that would be that.

Trill flitted into the room and took
in the sounds. The hiss of the teapots.

The chatter of fairies. Everyone was talking about the Oceanside Symphony, and about Bess's new painting. The sketch she had outlined was now a portrait and already hanging on a wall.

"Great work!" Beck told Bess, flying past the art-talent table.

"When is the symphony?" a sparrow man asked. "I can't wait!"

"I think we'll use fireflies for the finale," Fira told another light talent.

"Let's try a new pie recipe!" Dulcie called to the bakers in the kitchen. They were already preparing for the feast.

Just as Cleff had wanted, Bess's painting had gotten everyone excited. His idea had been a good one. What would he think of Trill's?

At the music-talent table, Cleff was bent over his scroll, scribbling more notes. Trill slipped in next to him and said, "Can I talk to you, Cleff?" It came out almost in a whisper.

Cleff was concentrating so hard, he

didn't hear. "If the drummers wear red, then the harpists should wear white," he muttered.

Trill cleared her throat. She'd have to speak more loudly. But before she could say anything more, Cleff reached for the serving bowl. It was empty.

Cleff frowned. "What's going on?" he asked Trill. "We always have sweet rolls with breakfast."

"The baking talents are getting ready for the symphony feast," she explained. "Maybe they don't have time."

Cleff liked things a certain way—the way he was used to. That was clear. Trill crossed her fingers. She hoped he wasn't too put out. "I'll bet the serving talents will bring rolls any minute."

Next to Cleff sat Ariette and Lyra. At the same exact moment, they picked up their teacups and took a sip.

Trill gathered her courage and went on. "But in the meantime . . ." She held out the paintbrushes. "C-c-could you listen to Cadence play the drums? Using these? Then you can hear how it sounds."

Ariette and Lyra both turned to Trill. "Playing the drums with paintbrushes!" they said together. "How—

"—fascinating!" said Ariette.

"—strange!" said Lyra at the same time.

Cleff set his fork and knife next to his plate so everything lined up perfectly. "No one's ever played the drums with paintbrushes," he said. "And there must be a good reason." He shook his head. "It's just not done."

More music talents were joining the table now. They all seemed interested.

Trill gazed down at her lap. Her cheeks flushed with embarrassment. What should she do? This could be important!

Finally, Trill looked up. Across the table, Cadence nodded. "B-b-but why not try something new?" Trill's voice was low. "Experiment?"

A serving talent placed fresh sweet rolls next to Cleff. "Ah! At last!" he crowed. He wasn't even listening.

"Why not experiment?" Trill said loudly.

Cleff stared at her, his hand stopped

in midair as he reached for a roll. Trill's glow flared, even in the bright sunshine.

"I—I—I mean, maybe we can experiment," she said more quietly. "We can try new sounds. Maybe even new instruments."

Trill lowered her eyes. In front of her were some cups. They were filled with different amounts of tea.

"Look!" Trill placed the cups in a row. Then, taking a knife, she struck them one by one. Each cup rang out with a different note. *Bong, bing, bing.*

"That's like a xylophone," Prilla called out from across the room. "I've seen Clumsies play them!"

"How about adding this to the concert?" Trill asked Cleff.

Together, the twins said, "That would be—

"—great!" said Ariette.

"—ridiculous!" Lyra said at the same time. She glared at her twin.

"I wouldn't call it ridiculous." Cleff leaned back in his chair. "But we have our own ways here. Traditional ways. And we *don't* use *cups* for instruments!"

The notes are so lovely, though, Trill thought. *They'd blend so well with the music.* She wanted so much for fairy music to be meaningful . . . for everyone to be moved.

Trill opened her mouth to protest, but no words came out. She couldn't disagree with Cleff. Not in front of everyone!

Just then, Tinker Bell flew in through an open window. She carried two saucer-shaped steel pots.

"New pots coming through!" she yelled. "Watch out. Dulcie needs these right away!"

A sudden thought struck Trill. If she could use teacups for instruments . . . what about pots?

Before she even realized it, she was fluttering over to Tink. "Can Dulcie wait just a minute?" she asked.

"What?" Tink said, surprised. Trill felt surprised, too. She'd never spoken up like this before—especially to a fairy as strong-minded as Tink.

"P-p-please?" Trill added. She held out her hands for the pots. Still taken aback, Tink gave them to her without a word.

Fairies turned in their seats to watch.

"If we just do this . . ." Trill's voice trailed off. She placed one pot on top of the other, open ends together. The pots formed a cylinder.

"Ta-da! A new kind of drum!" Trill struck the pots lightly. A sweet ringing tone swept across the room.

"Hey!" cried Cadence. "Do it again!" Cadence beat the table with a spoon while Ariette tapped the xylophone of cups.

A music talent named Jango grabbed two knives and used them as rhythm sticks. Another musician poured salt into two teacups and rattled them like

maracas. Someone else banged trays together for cymbals.

Trill moved in time to the music. It was all spur-of-the-moment. The music wasn't planned or studied. And it was beautiful.

"I'll make more pots for you!" Tink offered.

"They would be great for the concert," Cadence added.

"No, no, no!" Cleff's voice rose above the others. Everyone stopped. A hush fell over the tearoom.

"Whoever heard of a steel-pot drum? Or paintbrush drumsticks? Or a . . . a"—Cleff stood and pointed to the xylophone—"whatever you call that thing! I say the concert will go on as it always has. It will be the classic Oceanside Symphony. And it will be unchanged."

Every fairy in the room looked at Trill to see what she'd do next.

The music talent felt the familiar heat of embarrassment deepen her glow. She stepped back into the shadows.

Come on, Trill! she urged herself. *You can do it! You can answer him!*

If Trill didn't say anything now, Cleff would have his way. The symphony would continue in its ho-hum, already-been-done fashion. She had to speak up.

"Why c-c-can't there be new instruments?" Her voice wavered, but she went on. "And why can't there be new ways to play our old ones? Music is part of all

60

our lives. We should let it change and grow. We should try new things!"

"We should take these pots to the kitchen!" said Dulcie, bustling out.

Everyone laughed except the music talents. Trill stood silently on one side of their table, Cleff on the other. And neither one planned to move anytime soon.

6

Trill darted out of the Home Tree. She wanted to sit by the river and think.

"I can't believe I spoke up like that!" she said out loud as she flew through the courtyard. "In front of everyone!"

Was Cleff angry? Surprised? Trill didn't know. After Dulcie took the pots away, breakfast had ended. Fairies and sparrow men had scattered. Trill hadn't had a chance to talk to Cleff—even if she'd wanted to.

"Trill!" Cadence called out. She flew to her friend's side. "It's Lily's Arrival Day," she whispered. "All the music talents are going to her garden to surprise her. Can you come?"

Trill nodded. Of course she could! Sitting by the river could wait. No matter what else was happening, she didn't want to miss Lily's Arrival Day song.

Together, the friends flew to the garden. Trill saw that Cleff was already there, hiding behind a raspberry bush with Ariette and Lyra.

Trill pointed to a patch of daisies— far away from Cleff. "Let's hide there," she whispered to Cadence.

They waved to Fira, Beck, Prilla, and the other fairies, who were peeking out from plants and flowers all around the garden.

Everyone ducked back into hiding when Lily and Tink flew overhead.

"Let's try out this watering can right now," Tink was saying.

"Were you able to fix it?" Lily asked.

"I think so. I replaced the spout with a tin from a Clumsy can. The label said 'Peas Soaked in Water.' Now it should pour just fine."

The two fairies landed by a patch of silver bells. "My favorites!" said Tink. She and Lily bent down to smell the flowers. Behind Lily's back, Tink signaled to the hiding fairies.

Tiptoeing, the fairies and sparrow men crept from their spots.

Lily stood up. "Well, should we try the watering—"

"Hooray, hooray for Arrival Day!" all the fairies sang together.

Lily jumped, startled. The music talents pulled out their instruments from pouches and leaf-packs. Cadence rolled out her drum, which was hidden behind a shrub. Cleff held a mini-harp.

Then Beck waved to a group of crickets to whistle along. Everyone circled around Lily.

With a pang, Trill remembered she had no instrument. Her panpipes, her beloved panpipes, couldn't accompany the others.

All the fairies and sparrow men launched into the song:

"Hooray, hooray for Arrival Day!
Hooray, hooray for Arrival Day!
You are born from laughter
And a Never fairy ever after.
From the first sprinkling of dust,
You'll have magic you can trust.
Hooray, hooray for Arrival Day!
Hooray, hooray for Arrival Day!"

The song was so beautiful! Trill's fingers were itching to play. She couldn't just stand and listen. She needed an instrument. Any instrument! Then she spied a patch of clover just outside the garden hedge.

Clover! Trill remembered a field of clover not far from the river. Every time a breeze blew, the wind whistled through the flowers. It was music, pure and simple.

Would just a few sprigs make the same kind of sound?

Trill darted over to the patch and plucked some clover from the ground. Quickly, she fashioned a whistle.

TWEET! The sound was so surprising, everyone stopped singing.

All eyes turned toward Trill, who was still holding the clover to her mouth.

"Stop!" cried Pluck, a harvest-talent fairy. "What are you doing, Trill? That plant has three leaves. It's itchy ivy!"

Cadence inched away from Trill.

In a flash, Trill dropped the leaves. The last thing she wanted was a rash. She scratched her arm. Already, she felt itchy.

"Itchy ivy? Oh, no! There may be more!" a garden-talent fairy named Rosetta shouted in a panic. "It grows like crazy!"

Fairies fluttered in confusion. A baking talent carrying a tray of Arrival Day cupcakes bumped into Tinker Bell. Pink and yellow cupcakes flew everywhere.

"Hold on!" Lily called. "Calm down. It's not itchy ivy. It's only clover."

"It's not itchy ivy?" Beck repeated.

"Did you hear?" Cadence asked Jango. "Lily said it's okay."

"It's only clover! It's only clover!" Ariette and Lyra said together.

One by one, the fairies and sparrow men quieted down. They settled back on the ground.

"Pluck!" a sparrow man muttered. "What were you thinking?"

"Clover looks a lot like itchy ivy," Lily said, putting her arm around Pluck. "Anyone could make a mistake like that."

Cadence flitted over to Trill. "That clover made an amazing whistle."

Ariette, Jango, and a few others crowded closer, agreeing.

Trill sneaked a look at Cleff. He was standing off to the side, shaking his head.

"Whistles are a fairy tradition," he said, loudly enough for everyone to hear.

"They're made from blades of grass. It's just plain crazy to try to improve them. In fact, Never Land music doesn't need any improvements. Change can only cause trouble." He pointed at the ruined cupcakes on the ground.

Lyra flew next to Cleff. "I agree with Cleff."

Ariette flew next to Trill. "Well, I agree with Trill."

"You're wrong."

"No, *you're* wrong."

Other musicians chimed in. Their voices rose, louder and louder.

Trill hadn't meant to start an argument. She'd just wanted to join the song. But the way she'd felt at breakfast . . . and the way she felt now . . . were important.

Music shouldn't be stale. It should be alive. Changing.

Music expressed so many feelings! She couldn't bear for even the smallest bit to be stifled.

Trill listened to the others. She didn't trust herself to speak. Sure, she'd spoken out in the tearoom. But now, Cleff had voiced his disapproval for everyone to hear. What if she couldn't speak clearly? What if she stammered? And blushed?

Trill straightened her shoulders and wings. She stood tall, her head above the others.

Soon most of the fairies went their separate ways. But the music talents kept arguing. They argued as they left Lily's garden. They argued as they did chores. They argued as they sat in the tearoom, eating lunch.

As the day wore on, the bickering only got worse. No one could agree when to meet for a rehearsal. So they didn't.

Ariette wanted to help Beck train crickets for their symphony piece. But so did Lyra. When the twins saw each other, they both left. And the job went undone.

Some trumpet players finally did get together. But one made a face when another hit a sour note. The second musician stuffed an acorn into the first fairy's trumpet flower so she couldn't play.

The Oceanside Symphony would be the next night. A few fairies refused to perform if the music wasn't played the old way. Others vowed they'd play however they wanted.

"What do you think, Trill?" Jango came up to her in the late afternoon. "How about using spiderweb silk for harps, instead of silkworm silk?"

"Sounds good!" Trill said. "If the web is really sticky, the strings can stay right on the wooden frame. They won't even need sap!"

Trill flew off. But she was stopped a moment later by Ariette.

"I found these washed up on the beach!" Ariette held up two smooth pebbles. "We can string them together to make castanets. They'd sound different from the shells we always use!"

For hours, fairies had been seeking out Trill. They wanted her opinion on so many things! It was scary and exciting all at once. And she'd talked more than she ever had before.

She was needed in so many places, to answer so many questions! Trill didn't have time to check on her own panpipes.

Finally, in the early evening, Trill flew to Strad's workshop.

Strad was working busily, her head bent low as she sanded the bamboo panpipes. She looked up when she heard Trill come in.

"I'm still trying to fix your instrument," Strad told her. A frown crossed her face. "And I'm not sure I can finish in time." Not waiting for an answer, Strad went back to work.

Trill's heart sank, but she tiptoed out, not saying a word. Suddenly, Lyra and Ariette swept past Trill, quarreling loudly.

"Traditional!"

"New!"

"Traditional!"

"New!"

Trill groaned in dismay. *Everyone is arguing so much!* she thought. *And I still don't have an instrument!*

How would the musicians play together? And how would *she* play at all?

7

Trill flew up the Home Tree stairway to her room. Right by the door, she skidded to a stop.

"I've got it!" she almost shouted.

Trill had figured out one problem— what to do about her panpipes. She would make her own instrument again, this time for the Oceanside Symphony!

But she wouldn't use bamboo

shoots. That would be boring! She'd use something new and different. Why, it might be even better than her old instrument!

What could it be? Trill wondered. Reeds? They'd be hard to find on short notice. Plant stems? No, they'd wilt.

"Think, Trill!" she told herself. "Think!"

Twigs? No, they wouldn't work. Rolled-up flower petals? No again.

As she got ready for bed, Trill was still thinking. Maybe something that came from an animal. An eggshell? No, too fragile. But what about quills? From a porcupine!

The more she thought about it, the more sense it made. Quills were hollow.

She'd just get the quills in the morning. Then she'd be all set.

Trill slipped into bed and pulled the pussy-willow blanket over her shoulders.

But she couldn't rest quite yet. What about the other problem—the musicians fighting, old music versus new? Cadence and Ariette and many of the others were counting on her. Her! Shy, awkward Trill, who just wanted to play music and be left alone. How would she lead them? What should she do?

Trill tossed and turned for hours.

It wasn't until the sun rose over the meadow that she made a decision. She'd have to talk to Cleff. It would be difficult. And she'd really rather stay quiet. But somehow, she'd convince him that her way was the right way. Then he'd convince Lyra and the other musicians.

Ariette, Jango, and Cadence would have bushels of unique instruments in time for the symphony. The concert would feature these, and all-new, all-different music. It would be the most exciting symphony ever.

Trill drifted off to sleep. Just a few hours later, she woke. Hurriedly, she got dressed. Then she opened her door.

"Oh!" she gasped. Cleff stood right in front of her. His hand was raised, ready to knock on her door.

"You missed breakfast, Trill," he said. "And I wanted to talk to you."

"I—I—I wanted to talk to you, too," Trill told him.

Cleff nodded but went right on speaking. "I finally put two and two together. Your . . . ah . . . fascination with new music? It's all because you don't have your panpipes! You want to try something new because you don't have anything old! So I asked Strad to work all night on your panpipes. And she did it. She fixed them!"

Cleff held out Trill's instrument. "They're as good as ever. Ready to be used in the symphony tonight. You don't need any crazy drums or whistles! It will be music as it's meant to be played. Our tried-and-true program."

"My panpipes!" Trill's heart filled with joy. She reached for the instrument. As always, the pipes fit her hands perfectly. It felt so right to have them back. How would they sound?

Tootle-whoo. Whooo-toot. Lovely! Trill grinned, and she kept playing. For a moment she forgot about the concert. She forgot everything but the sweet, familiar sounds of her panpipes. *Tootle, whooooooo . . .*

"So, what do you think?" Cleff interrupted Trill's playing.

Thoughts of the concert came back to her.

"This is wonderful!" she told Cleff. "Just wonderful! But I still—"

"Cleff! Cleff!" Lyra raced down the hall. "Here you are! There's an emergency at the beach, right at the site of the symphony! Come quick!"

Before Trill could continue, Cleff took off. "See you tonight!" he called over his shoulder.

Trill was left alone, holding her panpipes. "Traditional," she said slowly. "Tried-and-true."

She felt very happy to have her panpipes back. But this symphony was an opportunity. A chance for all fairies and sparrow men to hear new music.

I'll still play the quill pipes, Trill decided. *Cadence and the others will still play their new instruments.*

And Cleff still needed to know.

Trill flew quickly to the shore. "Oh!" She came to a stop so suddenly, her heels dug into the sand.

Dozens of hermit crabs swarmed the beach. The decorating-talent fairies had already set up the concert spot. But the crabs were turning over chairs and knocking over tables put out for the feast. It looked as if a hurricane had swept across the sand.

Rani, a water-talent fairy, was there, and so was Beck, along with Cleff.

"I didn't mean for this to happen!" Rani said, tears streaming down her face. "I was helping the decoration talents by diving for pretty shells."

Trill nodded. Rani didn't have wings, so she was the only fairy who could swim.

"But now all these hermit crabs are here!" Rani sobbed.

"They're shell shopping," Beck explained. "They want to see if any of these snail shells can replace the ones they're outgrowing."

Trill heard the fluttering of wings. She looked up. Baking talents were delivering food now. As soon as a fairy set down a tray, hermit crabs scuttled over and rooted through the treats.

"They'll never leave now!" Cleff wrung his hands. "It's only a few hours to the concert!"

"I'll lead them away," Beck promised. "But we need to cover the food. And we'll have to move the shells, too."

Rani nodded. Decoration talents began sprinkling fairy dust on the shells so they'd be easier to carry. Cleff placed leaves over the trays, and Trill hurried to help. Meanwhile, Beck was herding the crabs to a large pile of driftwood.

It took a couple of hours, but everything was finally done. Cleff sighed. "Well, that's taken care of," he said. "The concert can go on as planned."

Trill stood at her full height. "Umm, maybe not *quite* as planned." Her voice quavered a bit. But she didn't stammer.

She quickly explained her idea for the porcupine quills and all the new instruments.

"The symphony can be special—unique!" she finished.

"Special?" Cliff scoffed. "I think it's special just the way it is. And as for porcupine quills . . ." Cleff's voice trailed off. "Why use something that's untested when you have perfectly good panpipes already? The whole thing is ridiculous, Trill. Listen to me. You can't do it."

"How can you say I can't do it?" asked Trill. Her voice held steady. "It's never even been tried."

Beck flew over to join them. "You're

thinking of using porcupine quills?" she asked. "It's true, the quills are hollow, like pipes. But I don't think it's a good idea, either. Getting the quills would be hard. Porcupines are prickly creatures. They can be very grouchy. It might be dangerous."

Trill didn't care.

Cleff and Beck kept talking. They were saying it wouldn't work. They were saying Trill could get hurt. But they were talking to one another. No one was paying attention to Trill.

She took one step away from them, then another. Beck and Cleff were caught up in their conversation. They didn't notice her leaving.

She'd sneak away right now. She'd

ask Cadence to organize the musicians, the ones who believed in new music. Then she'd find those porcupine quills.

Trill flew away from the beach . . . quickly, quietly, and unseen.

8

TRILL FOUND CADENCE and explained. Then she took off for the forest.

First things first, Trill thought. *I have to find a porcupine.*

Staying close to the ground, Trill flew from tree to tree. She searched in holes. She poked her head into dark places. She hunted under hanging branches.

Dusk was falling. It was getting hard

to see. Trill knew she didn't have much time. The concert would start soon.

But the darkness could be helpful. A porcupine might be going to sleep right about now. She could sneak up and take some quills without even waking him.

The sky turned darker. Shafts of moonlight filtered through the trees. Bits of music drifted on the breeze. Trill knew it was the music talents tuning up their instruments.

Maybe I should turn around, Trill thought as she peeked into a hollow log, *and*—

She stopped in midthought. There, all curled up, a porcupine slept. She flitted closer. *Zzzzz*. He was snoring. Perfect!

Trill flew into the log. She hovered in the air. As quick as a wink, she plucked one quill. Then she heaved it out of the log.

The porcupine twitched his nose.

Trill waited a moment. Then she pulled out another.

This is easy! she thought. *I'll do just one more. . . .*

Feeling a little too sure of herself, she hastily yanked out a third.

"*Eeee!*" The porcupine jerked awake. His quills bristled. Sensing danger, he twisted around. His back quills—the longest and sharpest ones—pointed right at Trill.

"Oh!" Trill gasped. Quills pressed closely on either side of her. She was pinned.

Too late, Trill realized that the porcupine hadn't been falling asleep at all. He'd been waking up!

Why, oh, why hadn't she listened to Beck? The animal talent had said lots of things about porcupines while she was talking to Cleff. Hadn't she said something about the animals being . . . nocturnal, was it? Did that mean they slept during the day and woke at night? It must!

Trill froze in fear. Moments passed. She felt the porcupine relax. Now she could see around his large body to his head. He was gnawing on a twig that was lying inside the log.

What would happen when he finished eating? He'd want to leave his den, of course.

He'd squeeze out of the hollow log. He'd press against the sides of the log to climb out. His quills would prick her wings!

"Help!" she cried. "Mr. Porcupine! There's a fairy here! I'm here!"

Trill shouted loud and strong, without any stutter at all. But the porcupine kept chewing as if he didn't hear.

Trill called out again and again. Then she fell silent. In the quiet, she heard a small noise. It sounded like the flutter of fairy wings. Could it be? Had a fairy heard her shouts? Was help on the way?

9

TRILL SQUINTED IN the darkness. Her glow had never been very bright. She could hardly see her own wings. But she sensed someone flying close. Was it Beck coming to her rescue?

"Is anyone there?" she called. She twisted around, hoping for a better view.

"Stop squirming! You'll make it more difficult."

Trill caught her breath. It was Cleff!
"O-o-okay," she said.

Trill held herself steady as Cleff
lifted one quill. He did it so gently,
the porcupine didn't notice. Then, still
holding that quill in place, Cleff pushed
down the one next to it.

"There's enough space for you to

fly!" Cleff's voice was strained with effort.

Trill slipped out unharmed. She darted up and away.

Free! she thought. *I'm free!*

She landed on top of the rock. A second later, Cleff flew over to stand next to her.

Trill smiled at Cleff. "I really appreciate—"

"How could you be so reckless?" he said angrily.

"What?" Trill stepped back.

"You risked your life!"

Trill ducked her head. "You didn't listen to me!" Cleff went on. "I'm in charge. And I told you not to do this."

Trill's glow blazed. She thought of

all the fairies who had asked *her* for advice. "You're in charge of the concert. But you're not in charge of me," she told Cleff.

A trumpet blared, and then the beat of drums echoed through the forest. The musicians were ready.

"I don't have time for this," Cleff said. "I have a symphony to lead!" In a flash, he was gone.

Trill gathered the quills. The new panpipes would have to wait. She needed to get to the concert, too.

Trill raced to the beach. She flew faster than she ever had before. She got there out of breath, with her curly hair in knots from the wind. But Cleff had beaten her. He stood on a shell, his back to the musicians. He was smiling at the audience.

"And so," he was saying, "the Oceanside Symphony begins!"

Trill eyed the musicians. Cadence had followed her instructions. She sat off to one side, along with Ariette and some others. They all held new instruments. But where was Jango? He was supposed to be playing his harp, with new spiderweb string.

Trill couldn't waste a minute wondering about Jango. She turned her attention to the other side of the orchestra. The music-talent fairies who agreed with Cleff were grouped together. They looked at Cleff, their traditional instruments ready.

Cleff faced his musicians and raised his twig-baton.

It was now or never. Trill had to act. She had to lead her orchestra! She might not have an instrument, but she did have a baton. She broke off a piece of quill.

She jumped onto the shell next to Cleff. Looking straight at him, she raised her baton.

Cleff's chin jutted out. His eyes narrowed. Ignoring Trill, he flicked his wrist. His musicians sounded their first note, then their second. Music streamed out into the clear moonlit night.

Cleff spread his arms, signaling a break in the piece.

"Now!" Trill told herself.

She nodded to her fairies and waved

the quill. Right away, her musicians began to play. They were fewer in number, but they played with all their hearts. New sounds, different music, echoed over the waves.

Trill caught her breath, and Cleff took over. His musicians stood up now, ready to play more loudly.

When Cleff paused, Trill's side came in. Then Cleff's side. Then Trill's. Each time, the musicians played more loudly. The bands battled on and on.

The music swelled. Neither side was resting. Everyone was playing at once. Frowning, their backs to one another, Trill and Cleff kept conducting.

Ta-da, ta-da. Ta-da, ta-ta-da. Notes melded together. *Boom, sweep, boom.*

The two types of music became one. *T-t-t-tweet, sh-shush, bing, boom, whooooo.* The music talents blended sounds unlike anything heard before.

Why, it's lovely, Trill thought. Her frown faded. Then it changed into a smile. Slowly, she turned toward Cleff. He was smiling, too!

Together, they led the orchestra. This was music at its best. All the musicians joined together, playing as one.

The piece ended. The audience rose into the air, clapping wildly.

"Bravo!" called Tink.

"Hooray for Cleff and Trill!" Beck shouted.

Trill reached for Cleff's hand. And together they bowed.

10

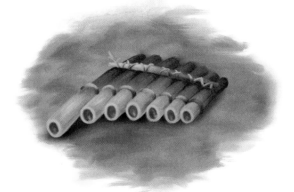

AFTER THE SYMPHONY, Trill glowed with pride. Fairies and sparrow men rushed to her side. Cleff was surrounded, too. In seconds, a sea of admirers separated the two musicians.

"Congratulations! That was so special! You did an amazing job!" fairies and sparrow men shouted out.

Trill gazed over everyone's heads.

Her eyes met Cleff's. She nodded, then made her way closer.

"Who'd have thought?" Cleff said with a smile. "Our symphony was a smashing success!"

Just then, Jango raced over. He was covered head to toe in stringy spiderweb.

"Did I miss it?" he panted loudly. "Is the concert over?"

"Yes!" Trill cried. "Where were you? What happened?"

"I went looking for a spiderweb, like you said, Trill. But the web was so sticky, I got caught! I just got out now!"

"Oh, it's all my fault," Trill groaned. She felt terrible.

But Jango was smiling.

"It's okay! I listened to the music.

I loved it!" He turned to Cleff. "And because I was listening, just listening, I came up with all these ideas for the next symphony. Can we talk later?"

Trill caught her breath. Would Cleff be willing to listen to someone else's ideas now? New ideas?

"Sure," said Cleff. "I'd be happy to." He grinned at Trill. "Sometimes it pays to experiment."

Trill grinned back. "And sometimes it doesn't pay at all." She rubbed her elbow, which was still a little sore from scraping against the porcupine's log.

"Sometimes things are done a certain way for a reason," Trill went on. "I took everything way too far. That clover could have been itchy ivy. And those porcupine quills . . ." Trill shivered. She could have been seriously hurt instead of having a scraped elbow.

She picked some web off Jango's wing. "Poor Jango. I gave you awful advice. You might have been stuck in that web for days!"

All around Trill, Jango, and Cleff, musicians hugged and chatted. Ariette and Lyra stood side by side. "I'd fly backward if I could," Ariette told Lyra.

"No, *I'd* fly backward," Lyra said to Ariette.

No one was angry. The argument had ended along with the concert.

"I guess both types of music have a place," Trill said in a loud, clear voice. "Both sides are right."

Fairies and sparrow men turned toward her, listening. And that was just fine with Trill. Sure, she'd made mistakes. And she'd probably make more. But she wouldn't feel embarrassed about speaking her mind. *Everyone's* ideas should be heard.

The next day, Trill led Cleff to the banks of the Wough River. They sat on the same birch tree where Trill had heard the nightingale's song.

"This is nice," Cleff told her. He turned his head, listening to the water's rumble. "Very nice."

A woodpecker perched on the next branch. *Tap, tap, tap. Rumble, rumble.* Trill and Cleff took in all the sounds. *Bzzz!* They jumped at the buzzing of a bee. Then they both smiled.

"I've been looking for you, Trill!" Just as on that other day, Beck was flying nearby.

"Really!" Trill called back, not hesitating a bit.

"They're over here!" Beck shouted to Strad. The instrument maker was flying more slowly. In her hand she had a bulky leaf-bag.

Cleff met the two fairies halfway. Then, at the same time, he, Strad, and Beck crowded around Trill and shouted, "Surprise!" Strad held out the bag.

"*Wh-wh-what?*" Trill couldn't figure out what was going on.

"This is for you," Cleff told Trill.

Cleff reached inside the bag and pulled out brand-new panpipes—made from porcupine quills.

"Beck found your quills and gave them to me," Strad told Trill. "I pulled a second all-nighter, making this instrument. But it was definitely worth it. I have to admit, it's another work of art. Try it out."

Trill took the panpipes in her hands. They weren't sharp at all. And they felt lighter than her old ones. Different. She blew across an opening. *Whoo!* The sound was different, too. More airy.

"I like it!" Cleff declared. "What about you?"

"Yes!" Trill said. And she did. Still, she couldn't help wondering—did everyone expect her to use these now, and forget about her old panpipes? She touched the instrument slung at her side.

Cleff chuckled. "Don't worry. You don't have to give up your old pipes."

Trill laughed. She'd have the best of everything, new and old.

"You can play either one at Fawn's Arrival Day celebration," Beck told Trill. "Everyone's meeting at the animal tunnel entrance."

"Let's get the musicians!" said Cleff.

Trill grinned. "And all the instruments. So we can play together."

They flew in opposite directions to gather their friends. Trill flew toward the mouth of Havendish Stream. Cleff flew toward the far corner of the orchard. But minutes later, everyone met by the tunnel—right in the middle.

Don't miss any of the magical
Disney Fairies chapter books!

Myka Finds Her Way

Myka had to get closer. She had to see what was
happening. She flew toward the noise and lights.
The rumblings turned to roars. The flashes grew
brighter.

Everything looked strange in the on-again,
off-again flare of light. *Boom!*

She saw a gnarled tree bent over, its bare
branches sweeping the ground. *Boom!* She spot-
ted a towering beehive. It swayed from the thick
trunk of a maple tree.

She swerved around it and kept flying.
Boom! The spooky light cast long shadows from
trees . . . plants . . . rocks. Everything seemed
different. But she was a scout. She had to keep
going.

Vidia Meets Her Match

Wisp's whole face lit up. "Race? With you? I'd love to!" she cried. "I hear you're the fastest fairy in Pixie Hollow."

"Mmm. Well, we'll see, won't we?" said Vidia.

Wisp's wings were already humming. "Where should we race?" she asked.

Vidia looked around. "From here to that tree," she decided. She pointed to a peach tree at the edge of the orchard. "To finish, touch the peach hanging from that low branch. Ready?"

Wisp nodded. The two got on their marks.

"Set . . . ," said Vidia.

They spread their wings.

"Go!"